Begat

Begat

By DC Fidler

DCFidler Publishing
2018

Published by DCFidler Publishing
1117 University Avenue, #505
Morgantown, WV 26505
DCFidlerpublishing@gmail.com

Printed in the United States of America
by Lulu Press, Inc.

This play is entirely a work of fiction.
Any resemblance to actual persons, living or dead,
is entirely coincidental.

ISBN: 978-0-9989729-4-7
Library of Congress Control Number: 2017919840

Setting

Raven, NC, Summer 2016. A small town with a mega-church outside of Charlotte, NC.

Reverend Loralee and Reverend Loudon Phillips' home.
   Living Room
   Kitchen
Chair and night table in spotlight
Pulpit in spotlight
Campfire in spotlight

Note: Kitchen and living room furniture and appliances can be placed on small turntables to simply rotate or roll on and off stage. Sets can be in limbo with only furniture.

Characters

Loralee Phillips	Middle-aged white woman, minister
Loudon Phillips	Middle-aged white man, minister
Simon Phillips	17-year-old white man, high school junior
Clarice Thompkins	19-year-old black woman, college sophomore engineering major
Howie Fitch	24-year-old white man, handyman

Note

In contrast to formal scripts for use in rehearsals, this is a book of the script, containing more stage directions to aid readers to envision what can be happening upon the stage. Most actors prefer few or no directions, allowing them to discover and create the lives of their characters.

Begat premiered on January 28, 2018 as a staged reading in Morgantown, WV with the following cast:

Loralee	Cynthia Ulrich
Loudon	Josh Brooks
Simon	Sean Marko
Clarice	Kayla Hudimac
Howie	Travis Teffner
Directed by	Travis Teffner

Thank you to the cast, Sandi Constantino-Thompson, and Joel Vogt for their helpful comments contributing to the script.

Scene One: Phillips' Living Room - Day

LORALEE, standing by the couch, hooks her black bra behind her back. HOWIE speaks from where he is lying on the floor, hidden behind the coffee table.

HOWIE: *(Yells.)* Come back down here!

LORALEE: I wuz down there plenty long.

HOWIE: *(Sits up, no shirt on.)* I'm ready to go agin.

LORALEE: Wish I wuz still twenty-four.

HOWIE: You ain't gonna send me home with blue balls now, is ya?

LORALEE: *(Puts on blouse.)* Simon gits home from school soon. Git dressed.

HOWIE: Well, hell fire. Let's not complicate Simon's life. *(Stands, wearing only boxers.)* Anyhow, I gotta go repair Sue Lynn Foster's dishwasher.

LORALEE: Put yer clothes on.

HOWIE: Ain't what'chu wuz beggin' me to do a minute ago. *(Puts on pants.)*

LORALEE: Is that all you gonna repair fer Sue Lynn? Her dishwasher?

HOWIE: Yes ma'am. Help out where I kin.

LORALEE: Exactly how many ladies'a my congregation do you "repair?"

HOWIE: Entire flock. Praise the Lord.

LORALEE: That's blasphemy.

HOWIE: I already got me a place reserved in hell. But if I remember right—and I do—jest a minute ago you wuz yellin', "hallelujahs."

LORALEE: Git dressed!

HOWIE: You deliverin' tonight's sermon?

LORALEE: Loudon's turn.

HOWIE: Yer better preachin' than him any ole day.

1

LORALEE: Lots'a people tell me that. "Loralee? We enjoy yer sermons way better than yer husband's." 'Specially televised night ones.

HOWIE: Guess what?

LORALEE: I fear guessin'.

HOWIE: When you night preach on TV?

LORALEE: Yeah?

HOWIE: I watch you up in my bedroom. My big-screen. Makes you life size.

LORALEE: Do I look good?

HOWIE: Pretty as a peach. Like yer there 'side me. Causin' me to re-live all the sweet things we done. So I—

(He gestures masturbating.)

LORALEE: Lord knows I ain't needin' to picture what yer doin' to yerself while I'm televisin'. And in the house with yer mama there.

HOWIE: She can't climb steps no more.

LORALEE: How come?

HOWIE: Three weeks ago. 'Nother minor stroke.

LORALEE: Oh. I am so sorry to learn that. She's so sweet.

HOWIE: So, I kin do anythin' I want up in my little ole room.

LORALEE: I hope she gits well'n walks in on you.

HOWIE: Won't be the first time.

LORALEE: Lord have mercy. That poor woman. Somebody should declare her a saint.

(HOWIE laughs.)

LORALEE: When I preach tomorrow night? I'll make up a special prayer fer her.

HOWIE: She'll appreciate that truly. I'll make sure she watches. Then I'll climb my stairs and *re-live!*

(Flips wrist back and forth in masturbatory fashion.)

LORALEE: *(Coughs a small cough and strokes her arm.)* Good Lord. I told ya to hurry.

HOWIE: I am, I am.

(Jerks hand faster.)

Hurry. Hurry. Faster. Faster.

LORALEE: Buckle them britches and git out 'fore you drive me plum insane.

HOWIE: Yes ma'am. Right away, ma'am.

LORALEE: *(Eyes HOWIE as he stretches to put on T-shirt.)* You been workin' out extra?

HOWIE: Usual. Why?

LORALEE: You look ... good.

HOWIE: Try to.

LORALEE: You datin' anybody serious?

HOWIE: Now why would I go and do that?

LORALEE: Maybe—I don't know—Some girl you don't never tell me 'bout.

HOWIE: Ain't got time fer "serious." Got a career to mind.

LORALEE: Yer the best carpenter in Raven. What'chu need with a career?

HOWIE: Electric wirin'. Plumbin'. Night classes.

LORALEE: Night school? Huh. If that's what you de-sire—wirin' and plumbin'. But how is it, if you attend them night classes, you watch Loudon and I preach at night?

HOWIE: I don't watch. Not even Sunday mornin's.

LORALEE: That hurt my fillin's. Why'chu lie you watch us?

HOWIE: So I kin talk dirty at ya.

(Massages LORALEE'S shoulders.)

LORALEE: *(Pouting.)* Nobody give you permission to talk dirty to me.

HOWIE: I like turnin' you on.

LORALEE: Dirty talk don't turn me on. It turns my stomach.

HOWIE: Little chill bumps on yer skinny arms. Throat gits dry and you start them little coughin' spells. The way you press yer cute little tongue right here against yer upper lip.

LORALEE: Back in high school? I wuz a actress.

HOWIE: You? Actin'?

LORALEE: Won me a class award.

HOWIE: Oh. So, you jest act turned on. Uh huh. Jest like you act pure and saint-like on TV.

LORALEE: My preachin' ain't actin'.

3

HOWIE: Uh huh.
LORALEE: That's cuz ...
(Shakes off thought.)
HOWIE: Cuz what?
LORALEE: *(Pause.)* Cuz the Lord moves me.
HOWIE: Uh huh. The Lord. Right.
LORALEE: Shouldn't you be headin' to Sue Lynn's? Clear a load'a her dirty dishes. Or wuz servicin' her another lie designed fer my benefit?
HOWIE: Maybe. Maybe not.

(SIMON enters through front door.)

HOWIE: Simon! Hey boy! Me and yer old lady wuz jest talkin' 'bout'cha.
LORALEE: Why are you home way early, honey?
SIMON: Joey Mozella had a knife at school.
HOWIE: A honest to gosh knife? Didn't know the girlie boy had it in'im.
SIMON: Boy Scout. Swiss Army. Forgot it was in his pocket. Stupid.
HOWIE: Hell yeah, he's stupid. When I used to go to school, I carried me a twelve-inch huntin' knife. Real man's knife. I bet Ms. Phillips, when you wuz in school—way, way back—kids toted muskets. Or wuz it tomahawks?
LORALEE: Thank you fer repairin' my oven, Mr. Fitch.
HOWIE: Guarantee it'll heat up real fine now. Steady glowin' heat.
LORALEE: How much did you say I owe you?
HOWIE: Well now. Helpin' you wuz such a pleasure, I'd feel plum guilty gittin' paid fer usin' my God-give talents.
LORALEE: Mail me yer over-chargin' bill.
HOWIE: If I can service anything else fer ya, I'll drop what it is I'm doin' and race right over.
LORALEE: Simon? You need me to fix ya a pimento-cheese sandwich or anything, honey?
SIMON: No, thank you.

4

LORALEE: Glass'a sweet tea?
SIMON: No, ma'am.
HOWIE: Well ...
   (Awkward pause.)
   See you on the field, bat boy. Keep care'a yer body,
   hear? Wrist action is a God send. In so many, many
   ways. Pitchin'? All about ...
   (Flexes wrist.)
   wrist action.
   (Slaps SIMON on shoulder and walks toward front door.)
   (SIMON frowns and shrugs the shoulder HOWIE patted.)
LORALEE: Oh! Mr. Fitch? Didn't you park out back, sir? By
   our kitchen door?
HOWIE: Darn if I didn't. Lady. Gentleman.
   (Exits through house.)
SIMON: What a creep.
LORALEE: Jest a bigmouth know-it-all.
SIMON: I heard he's in the klan.
LORALEE: The klan?! Gracious! Now, who gone and made
   up dangerous trash about poor, simple Howie?
SIMON: The guys.
LORALEE: That's unbecomin' y'all boys. Don't be pleasin'
   the devil with idle chatter. We got plenty enough
   troubles.
SIMON: Mom, it's a known fact his uncle and brother are in
   the klan.
LORALEE: His uncle comes to church regular now and his
   brother's in prison.
SIMON: Whatever.
LORALEE: Joey didn't threaten nobody, did he?
SIMON: Really, Mom? Joey?
LORALEE: I didn't think so. But he is . . .
   (Whispers.)
   dark skinned.
SIMON: Italian. So what?
LORALEE: I jest meant he might git bullied. Don't go
   throwin' a hissy fit like I'm some racist. I hate when you
   and yer daddy act like I am.

(SIMON sighs and rolls eyes.)
LORALEE: Joey ain't in trouble, is he?
SIMON: Police had him spread eagle on the floor. Handcuffed. Then ran us off. I gotta grab my glove. Bolt for practice.
(He exits as LORALEE primps before the mirror, putting on lipstick.)
LORALEE: "Muskets." "Tomahawks." Sue Lynn's a heck'a lot older'n me. Seventeen months.

(SIMON returns from bedroom and hurries to front door.)

LORALEE: Wait! Ain't you forgittin' somethin'?
(She points at her cheek. SIMON sighs and kisses her on cheek.)
LORALEE: Praise the Lord.
SIMON: Yeah. That. Whatever.
LORALEE: You are full of rudeness today, Simon Alfred Phillips.

(SIMON hurriedly exits as LORALEE primps more and then straightens couch cushions.)

(Sound of doorbell.)

LORALEE: Lord, please don't let that be Howie comin' back fer seconds.
(Opening the door.)
If you think fer one minute—

(CLARICE is standing with a small, orange-wrapped package.)

LORALEE: Oh ... Uh, kin I help you?
CLARICE: Mrs. Phillips?
LORALEE: Yes. I'm Mrs. *Reverend* Phillips. And who might you be?

CLARICE: Nice to meet you. My name is Clarice Thompkins.

LORALEE: Are you sellin' somethin'? Cuz if you are? We don't buy from door-to-door people. Nobody livin' in this part'a Raven does.

CLARICE: Oh no, no. I'm not selling anything.

LORALEE: Then what is it you want?

CLARICE: My mother ...

(Pulls paper from purse.)

My mother gave me Reverend Phillips' address.

LORALEE: Well, Reverend Phillips is down at the church. Raven Christian? He takes care'a all charities outta our offices.

CLARICE: Oh no. I'm not here for a charity.

LORALEE: Then what is yer business? I got lots to do.

CLARICE: My mother asked that I look him up.

LORALEE: I clearly stated, "The Reverend is down at the church." He takes care'a all business down there. Not from our home. This is our personal space.

CLARICE: My visit is personal. May I come in?

LORALEE: Into our house? You are a complete stranger.

CLARICE: Mom knew Reverend Phillips very well. She never missed his broadcasts.

LORALEE: The Reverend comes through that TV very personally. Everybody feels loved by him. That's his gift—Mine, too.

CLARICE: We knew him in person.

LORALEE: Are you members of our congregation? I don't recall yer face.

CLARICE: We're from Raleigh.

LORALEE: Raleigh? Well, it's less'n three-hours from there to here. You and yer mama should sign up. Rayvon? My husband's assistant? Has stacks'a applications. *At* the church.

CLARICE: My mother died.

LORALEE: Oh ... I'm sorry to learn that. Sorry fer yer loss. Well ... I'm sure she's with Jesus now. Praise the Lord.

CLARICE: Could I have a drink of water or something? I took a taxi from Raleigh.

LORALEE: Three hours in a taxi?

CLARICE: The driver's air conditioning broke.

LORALEE: It's hot as you know where outside.

CLARICE: Of course, it would be my luck to summon the only blistering hot taxi during record-breaking heat. *(Indicates she wants to enter.)* May I?

LORALEE: Uh ...
(Leans out door and looks to see if anyone is watching.) I suppose so. Hurry in.
(Motions for CLARICE to enter, who pulls roller suitcase into doorway.)

LORALEE: You brought yer belongin's?

CLARICE: I'm on summer break.

LORALEE: You ain't plannin' on stayin' here!

CLARICE: To be honest, I don't know what I'm planning.

LORALEE: You hold it right there! I'm callin' Loudon.
(Marches to phone.)

CLARICE: Should I stand here in the door? Where your neighbors might see me?

LORALEE: There's no reason to be pert, young lady. You jest ... jest come in.
(Calls on living-room phone.)
And shut that door!
(CLARICE closes door.)

LORALEE: Hi, Angel. Is Loudon there? ... No. I cannot wait. Tell'im it's urgent.
(Eyes CLARICE examining objects in room.)
Loudon! There's a ... girl nosin' 'round our livin' room, who come to our front door sayin' her deceased mama asked her to seek you out ... Two minutes ago. Draggin' her big suitcase.
(To CLARICE.)
Sugar? What's yer name agin?

CLARICE: Clarice. Clarice Tom—

8

LORALEE: Clarice! ... What?! ... Fine.
(Holds phone out for CLARICE.)
He wants to have a word with you.
CLARICE: *(Accepts phone.)* Hello ... Fine, Reverend ... I'm saddened to tell you, she died a month ago. I didn't have your personal telephone number, so ... Yes, sir. Her body just gave out after a bad infection. She knew she was dying. She gave me a package to give to you. College is out for the summer, so I ... Yes, sir. All As. I love engineering ... Thank you. I took a taxi. Mother wrote your home address for me ... Yes, sir. I'll wait. Thank you, sir.
(Hangs up phone.)
LORALEE: What the ... ? I wuz *not* finished talkin' to my husband!
CLARICE: He hung up.
LORALEE: *He* hung up? Well! ... I take it yer mama knew my husband rather well.
CLARICE: Since elementary school. May I have a glass of water? Please?
LORALEE: Stay there. I'll git you a paper cup'a water.
(She exits to kitchen.)

(Lights to black.)

Scene Two: Phillips' Living Room - Day

LORALEE, sitting in a chair, taps her fingers and loudly sighs time to time. CLARICE, sitting on the couch, is absorbed reading a book.

LORALEE: *(Paces.)* I don't know what's takin'im so long.

(LOUDON enters front door as LORALEE watches.)

LOUDON: Clarice!
CLARICE: *(Running to LOUDON.)* Reverend Phillips!
(They hug tightly as LORALEE uncomfortably looks away.)
LOUDON: It is so wonderful to see you.
CLARICE: You, too.
LOUDON: Look how magnificent you are growing up. Wow!
CLARICE: University life agrees with me.
LOUDON: Absolutely, it does. I am so heartbroken about poor Chris Ann. What an outstanding lady.
CLARICE: Thank you. She contracted a strange infection that her doctors never could identify.
LOUDON: Oh my. How long was she sick?
CLARICE: A few weeks.
LOUDON: Oh my golly. I pray she didn't suffer greatly.
CLARICE: Very little actually. She gradually grew weaker until—
LORALEE: Well! Praise the Lord for that!
LOUDON: Oh. Sorry. Loralee? This is Clarice. Clarice? This—
LORALEE: Yes. We met.
LOUDON: Clarice's mother and I were good friends.
LORALEE: I'm delighted to learn that fact.
LOUDON: Yes, uh, I trust Loralee took good care of you.
CLARICE: Yes, sir. She served me a paper cup of water.
LORALEE: Honey? May I talk with you?
LOUDON: Of course.

LORALEE: Alone?

LOUDON: Oh ... Certainly. Uh, Clarice? Could you please excuse us for a moment?

LORALEE: You can wait in our family room. Through that door, down the hall, fifth room on the left. Don't go in any'a the other rooms.

(CLARICE nods and exits.)

LOUDON: That was rather curt.

LORALEE: Who is that girl? Who the heck is Chris Ann?

LOUDON: Chris Ann's Clarice's mother. Deceased mot—

LORALEE: I know that!

LOUDON: Sorry.

LORALEE: You never mentioned you had a Chris-Ann woman friend.

LOUDON: Half of the people in our congregation are women.

LORALEE: Not with daughters fallin' at yer feet like some kinda relations.

LOUDON: Oh, for gosh sakes.

LORALEE: All them trips to Raleigh? Church business?

LOUDON: Church business.

LORALEE: And on jest how many'a them "business" trips did you visit *Chris Ann*?

LOUDON: Once, maybe twice a year.

LORALEE: Oh really. Funny you never mentioned visits with "Chris Ann" to me.

LOUDON: I mentioned Ms. Tompkins' name to you numerous times. She donated money to build our church nursery.

LORALEE: What else did she "donate?"

LOUDON: Jealousy is unattractive on you.

LORALEE: I am not jealous. I am deceived.

LOUDON: Well, calm your head.

LORALEE: I'm not jealous!

LOUDON: You're the most easily jealous person ever existed.

LORALEE: Am not!

LOUDON: Martha Beymer?

LORALEE: She kisses you on the lips.

LOUDON: Like a grandmother kissing her grandson. She's eighty-four.

LORALEE: You don't see me kissing eighty-four-year-old men.

LOUDON: *(Mumbles.)* They're scared of you.

LORALEE: What was that?!

LOUDON: I said, you give'em the cold shoulder.

(SIMON enters through front door.)

LORALEE: *(Yells.)* I thought you had baseball practice!

SIMON: What did I do wrong?

(LORALEE sighs dramatically and turns her back on SIMON.)

SIMON: The ball park, the swimming pool, the gym, all on lock down because Joey brought his Boy Scout knife to school. Pardon me for coming back to the place where I live.

(Exits to bedrooms.)

LOUDON: Joey Mozella took a knife to school?

LORALEE: Don't change the subject.

LOUDON: What is it you want to know? Ask me. Any and every question churning in your hot head.

LORALEE: My head is calm now. I don't need to know nothin'.

LOUDON: Was I in love with Chris Ann? Yes. As friends love. Did I make love to Chris Ann? No. Did we kiss? No. Foreplay? No. Sleep in the same bed? No. Laugh together? Yes. Delightful laughing.

LORALEE: All right, all right. I git the picture.

LOUDON: You never get the picture.

(LORALEE pouts.)

LOUDON: That girl, young woman in there just lost her mother. She's alone in this world.

LORALEE: Where's her father?

LOUDON: She never knew ... her other parent.

LORALEE: Sounds like trash to me.

LOUDON: God almighty. Clarice is a straight-A engineering student. Full scholarship. Her mother was a highly recognized social worker. Set up award-winning preschool programs for disadvantaged children across the nation.

LORALEE: Well! Sounds like you and Chris Ann wuz jest made fer each other. Since elementary school.

LOUDON: What?

LORALEE: That academic superstar invadin' our home said you and her mama wuz friends way back in elementary school.

LOUDON: She said that?

LORALEE: Wuz you?

LOUDON: Uh ...

LORALEE: Either you wuz friends in elementary school or you wudn't. Yes or no?

LOUDON: We attended the same school, but I didn't know ... a Chris Ann back then.

LORALEE: Uh huh. Sounds peculiar to me.

LOUDON: I did *not* know Chris Ann in elementary school. Not in middle school. Not in high school.

LORALEE: And you got together way over in Raleigh how? Drove to her house one day, knocked on her door and said, "Well, Chris Ann honey. You don't know me, but I do believe we attended elementary school together." Or did she call you up? Looked ya up in her yearbook. Or cornered you at one'a them school reunion kinda flare ups.

LOUDON: There's no sense trying to talk reason with you.

LORALEE: I'm full'a reason. You jest don't got reasonable answers. Heck yeah my gears is spinnin' now. Outta orbit. Why don't you go socialize some more with that genius little girl? See what reasons you two can invent. I'm goin' to church and pray fer both yer souls. Light candles fer ya. I'll see you on set. Yer night to preach. I can hardly wait to hear—what is it you call'em?

13

Metaphors? That's it. What *metaphors* you come up with tonight.

(She exits. LOUDON checks his phone.)

LOUDON: Thunderstorms late tonight. I'll park my car outside for a power wash.

(As LOUDON pours a drink, SIMON enters.)

SIMON: You two finished fighting?

LOUDON: Oh. I was clarifying a complex situation for your mother.

SIMON: How'd that go for you?

LOUDON: She's lighting candles and praying.

SIMON: You must be in deep doo-doo.

LOUDON: She'll be fine.

SIMON: Who's the girl sitting in our family room?

LOUDON: She's uh ... uh ...

SIMON: The complex situation?

LOUDON: Yeah.

SIMON: She's really hot. I'll go introduce myself.

LOUDON: Wait ...

(SIMON exits. LOUDON downs his drink.)

(Lights to black.)

Scene Three: Phillips' Living Room - Night

SIMON spreads a camping tent on the floor and begins tying short lines to the tent tags. CLARICE enters and observes. SIMON becomes aware he is being watched.

SIMON: I'm tying lines to run from my tent to the stakes, so I won't have to add them after the tent is up.

CLARICE: I camp.

SIMON: Good.

(Hands lines to CLARICE.)

Tie that side.

(CLARICE gets on knees and ties lines.)

SIMON: Where do you camp?

CLARICE: Colorado.

SIMON: I thought you lived in Raleigh.

CLARICE: University adventure club. We camp out of state twice a year.

SIMON: After senior year, I'm trading in this hole of a place for college. Never look back. Do you ever camp closer than Colorado?

CLARICE: My neighbors used to invite me to camp with them up at Grandfather Mountain, Linville, that area. Once at the beach.

SIMON: Someday I'll camp in Colorado, Utah, Wyoming.

CLARICE: Go in summer. I froze my butt off.

SIMON: I like cold. Snow camping.

CLARICE: Snow? You're insane.

SIMON: Yep. It is genetic.

CLARICE: I didn't mean that you're actually insane.

SIMON: I meant it.

CLARICE: *(Pause.)* Your mother doesn't like me.

SIMON: She's racist.

CLARICE: Wow! That's to the point.

SIMON: I have a nasty habit of being honest.

CLARICE: Your dad's not racist.

SIMON: They grew up on different sides of the track.

CLARICE: What's that mean?

SIMON: You sure you're from the South?
CLARICE: We moved around. Mom's work.
SIMON: Where?
CLARICE: New York. DC. San Diego. Miami six months.
SIMON: Cities.
CLARICE: Then Raleigh.
SIMON: Small city.
CLARICE: What about you?
SIMON: No cities. Raven. Population 2,051. Actually less, but our mayor won't replace the sign. Losing population would taint her reputation.
CLARICE: 2,051. Bet your parents' church is twice that size.
SIMON: Seats three-point-two times as many.
CLARICE: Specific.
SIMON: Mom sucks at math, but she sure can count church members. Dad will inform you about weather more than any human cares to know, Mom about tithing members.
CLARICE: Who do you usually camp with?
SIMON: My black lab.
CLARICE: A dog?
SIMON: Buster.
CLARICE: No people?
SIMON: Nope.
CLARICE: I'd be scared to camp alone.
SIMON: I don't camp alone. I have Buster.
CLARICE: Oh. Yeah. Sure.
(They tie in silence.)
CLARICE: What will your mom do when she learns you and your dad invited me to stay over?
SIMON: Pout.
CLARICE: That's it?
SIMON: Pretend to be polite, large doses of resentment oozing through.
CLARICE: Do you think she believes your dad was having an affair with my mom?

SIMON: You're pretty much to the point, yourself. Absolutely she does.

CLARICE: They weren't.

SIMON: How do you know?

CLARICE: Just ... know.

SIMON: Good.

CLARICE: *(Pause.)* Mom couldn't.

SIMON: Couldn't have an affair?

CLARICE: Medical reasons.

SIMON: Hand me the tie by your foot.

(CLARICE hands tie to SIMON and watches him tie it.)

CLARICE: You aren't curious?

SIMON: About?

CLARICE: Mom's medical reasons.

SIMON: If you want me to know, you'll tell me.

CLARICE: Someday.

SIMON: I'll be here to listen.

CLARICE: You're like your father. Not your mother.

SIMON: God, I hope I'm not like her.

CLARICE: Not racist.

SIMON: Everybody's racist.

CLARICE: I'm not.

SIMON: Everyone is. Hand me that last one.

(CLARICE hands tie to SIMON.)

CLARICE: Do you attend their sermons?

SIMON: For real?

(Shakes head and snickers.)

CLARICE: I watched once. Mom watched often. Well, when your dad preached.

SIMON: Sounds like my dad and your mom were tight.

CLARICE: I liked your dad's visits. Read all of *Treasure Island* to me. One chapter per visit.

SIMON: He read stories to you when you were in high school?

CLARICE: Second grade.

SIMON: That far back. Huh.

CLARICE: Before Mom's job required us to travel.

SIMON: Did he use to stay over night?

CLARICE: In our guest room. If that's what you're asking.
SIMON: I was.
CLARICE: My mom would never—you know.
SIMON: They're all tied. Help me fold it.
(They fold tent as they talk.)
SIMON: No sex. Huh. So, what brought them together?
CLARICE: Doesn't have to be sex.
SIMON: Of course not.
CLARICE: School. Friendship.
SIMON: Duke?
CLARICE: Before college. Elementary, high school.
SIMON: No shit. My old man always claimed he was way too shy to ask girls out.
CLARICE: Not dating. Friends.
SIMON: Oh. Right. Boy-and-girl hanging out in small-town, 1990s North Carolina. Everybody did that. The 90s celibate revolution.
CLARICE: Okay, okay. I never asked. Chose not to think about it.
SIMON: Now you can torture yourself thinking about it.
CLARICE: I prefer not to.
(SIMON stuffs folded tent into bag.)
CLARICE: Are you going camping soon?
SIMON: I gotta check with Buster.
CLARICE: Does "Buster" maintain a heavy schedule?
SIMON: Girl-dog friends, bitches all over the county. They just hang out. No sex. Small-town, North Carolina dogs. Celibate.
CLARICE: You're making fun of me.
SIMON: You think?
CLARICE: You're not like guys in Raleigh.
SIMON: You're not like girls I met who lived in Miami six months.
CLARICE: Do you want to go out? Grab a bite? Walk?
SIMON: You asking me out?
CLARICE: A girl asking a boy?
SIMON: Everyone's sexist.

CLARICE: Yes or no?
SIMON: Absolutely ... Celibate walking.
CLARICE: Whatever.

(Lights to black.)

Scene Four: Phillips' Living Room - Night

LOUDON and LORALEE enter front door. LORALEE marches farther into house as LOUDON checks weather on phone.

LORALEE: *(Yells off stage.)* Simon? ... Simon? . . .
(Re-enters.)
Okay. Where are they?
LOUDON: Cool front. Dropping unusually low later: sixty-two. But for now, a comfortable seventy-eight. I imagine they took Buster for a walk.
LORALEE: A colored girl and a white boy walking in this neighborhood at night?
LOUDON: Trailing an old black dog.
LORALEE: This isn't funny.
LOUDON: Not in your world.
LORALEE: You and yer almighty-world, university-divinity major.
LOUDON: Degree.
LORALEE: College roommate Will marryin' that stuck-up, oriental, Chinese girl.
LOUDON: Her parents were from South Korea.
LORALEE: Not to mention yer on-the-side Raleigh church business.
LOUDON: My what?
LORALEE: Colored woman Chris Ann.
LOUDON: Chris Ann and I never went together. And? She's white.
LORALEE: White?
LOUDON: Wouldn't matter if she were purple. She was nice.
LORALEE: How then is Clarice ... you know.
LOUDON: I'm guessing at least one of her parents was some other color. What's your theory?
LORALEE: I jest thought that ...
LOUDON: Yes?
LORALEE: That . . .

LOUDON: That I was Clarice's father?

LORALEE: No, no. That never crossed my mind.

LOUDON: Yeah. Right.

LORALEE: I can't figure out who begat who in the Bible, much less who you begat. She acts like yer her daddy or somethin'.

LOUDON: A family friend. She acts like I'm a family friend.

LORALEE: This has been one traumatic day fer me.

LOUDON: You make all your days traumatic.

LORALEE: You and Simon shove me into traumas. I need a drink.

LOUDON: Me, too.

LORALEE: Set there. I'll git ya one.

(She grabs two bottles of beer from a mini-bar fridge.) Here.

LOUDON: I was thinking of scotch.

LORALEE: Pour it yerself.

(She sits and drinks as LOUDON pours himself a scotch.)

LOUDON: That was an emotionally draining sermon. One of my best if I do say so. Tolerance. Acceptance. What did you think?

LORALEE: I didn't hear a word'a it.

LOUDON: Simmering in your own sauces.

LORALEE: You don't think they'll kiss out in public, do ya?

LOUDON: An after-sex kiss?

LORALEE: Why is it you and Simon delight in tormentin' me so?

LOUDON: You reward us with high drama.

LORALEE: Cuz I inherited my daddy's hot streak.

LOUDON: That you did.

LORALEE: Tobacco farmers *had* to be hot headed or—

LOUDON: *(Disinterested, rote, rapid monotone.)* Or they got run over. You were stronger than your four brothers put together. The reason your daddy wanted you to take over the farm and—

LORALEE: But the Lord called me.

LOUDON: *(Resigned.)* Yes, he did.

LORALEE: Why do you detest my stories?

LOUDON: I have them so memorized I dream them.

LORALEE: Sweet dreams?

(She tries to kiss LOUDON but he avoids her.)

LOUDON: Sure. Sweet.

LORALEE: I can tell when yer fibbin'.

LOUDON: Are you going to leave it alone or interrogate our guest about the colors of her parents?

LORALEE: Did you love her lots? More than me?

LOUDON: Chris Ann was a friend. You and I had two children together.

(LORALEE goes to bar, pours herself a shot of gin and downs it in one gulp.)

LORALEE: I didn't hear nothin' 'bout "love" in yer justification.

LOUDON: I've never seen you swig gin. Terrible idea.

LORALEE: *(Pause.)* Tomorrow? Teresa would'a turned fourteen.

LOUDON: Fourteen. Yes.

(He sips.)

LORALEE: *(Pause.)* I bought us a wreath to take to the cemetery. Celebrate her birthday. White roses with a border of baby's breath. What she'd planned fer her confirmation party.

LOUDON: I'm staying here.

LORALEE: What? ... You attended last year. Said it wuz important.

(LOUDON does not respond.)

LORALEE: Mommy and Daddy are drivin' up from Goldsboro to meet us at the cemetery. Eat barbecue at Sonny's.

LOUDON: Right on schedule to hit us up for money.

LORALEE: My hard-earned money. Fine. You and Simon stay put and entertain Clarice. She acts like yer baby daughter anyhow. No reason to be rememberin' yer real daughter. I swear.

(She exits. Sounds of dog barking outside with SIMON and CLARICE laughing. LOUDON listens, sips, and then checks his phone.)

LOUDON: Yep. The high pressure's moving up. Shoving hotter weather our way.

(Lights to black.)

Scene Five: Phillips' Kitchen - Day

LORALEE, eating a pastry, paces as she talks on phone.

LORALEE: No, Ernie. When the choir starts quiet hummin', that's when I enter. Not before. And as I do, I want them lights to switch over to blue ... No, no! That wuz puke green! I want angelic blue. Purity. Saint—ness, whatever. And inform the choir no men's voices. Jest women. Git it right. Oh. And convey to Rodney I don't want no American flag on top. I want the church flag on top. Church is the most highest callin'.
(Ends call and yells into house.)
Simon! ... Simon! ...

(CLARICE enters wearing a bathrobe and sipping coffee.)

CLARICE: He's out jogging.
LORALEE: How in tarnation do you know?
CLARICE: Uh, I came into the kitchen to make coffee. He was in here warming up.
LORALEE: This isn't working.
CLARICE: What isn't working?
LORALEE: You nosin' 'round knowin' intimate details 'bout my family.
CLARICE: Jogging?
LORALEE: Everthin'!
CLARICE: Sorry.
(Pours more coffee into her cup.)
LORALEE: I gotta git over to the rectory.
CLARICE: I thought rectories were where ministers' families lived.
LORALEE: Well, you musta thought wrong, now didn't ya?
CLARICE: Our Episcopal priest and his family—
LORALEE: *(Yells.)* We're not Episcopals! We're Christians!
CLARICE: I'll finish my coffee in my room.
LORALEE: You jest do that, Princess.

(CLARICE exits.)
LORALEE: *(Mocks CLARICE.)* "My Episcopal priest."
(She calls on phone.)
Ellen? I changed my mind. I need white flowers linin'
my path to the pulpit. Ernie changed the lightin' to
blue. Blue on yellow flowers? 'Xactly. Sick. 'Specially on
TV. Most'a our revenue comes from TV members. I'll
drop in early and make sure ya got it right.
(Ends call.)
Now, where's my readin' glasses? I jest had'em.
(Yells.)
Clarice? Did you steal my readers? ...
(To self.)
Little brat.
(Finds glasses.)
Oh. She must'a moved'em jest to spite me.
(Puts on glasses and looks at notebook.)
Music, lights, flowers, organist—Darn it! Organist!
(Calls on phone.)
Charles? Swap out Mae Lynn for Dalton on the organ.

(SIMON hurriedly enters, sweaty, out of breath. He shuffles to the refrigerator and pours chilled water into a glass and gulps.)

LORALEE: She rushes my entrance no matter how much I
yell at her. Dalton has intelligence. Mae Lynn weren't
blessed with none. Now, I'm countin' on ya.
(Ends call and reads from notebook.)
Flowers, organist, programs—Don't gulp like that!
You'll spit up all over my kitchen.
SIMON: *(Burps.)* No, I won't.
LORALEE: Fine. You kin clean it up.
SIMON: When was the last time I "spit up" on your kitchen
floor? When I was one?
LORALEE: Well, you come close lots. And you exercise in
my livin' room. Sweat all over my 'spensive rugs. We
built ya a gym.

SIMON: I like the living room. It doesn't have cartoon ducks on the walls.
(He gulps more water.)
LORALEE: I swanee. Hurry up and shower 'fore school.
SIMON: The last day of school was Wednesday. Thanks to Joey, we were on lock down.
LORALEE: Finished fer the year? I don't remember no junior-senior prom.
SIMON: I skipped it.
LORALEE: Skipped? Who skips their junior-senior—
SIMON: Me.
LORALEE: Yer the school's star pitcher.
SIMON: Mom, Mom. I don't pitch for RHS. I pitch for the county league. Summer league?
(He exits.)
LORALEE: *(Yells.)* You should pitch fer yer school! I'll call'em and tell'em so!

(LOUDON enters while dressing.)

LORALEE: Where you headed?
LOUDON: The bank. Review loan plans for our third-floor classroom extension.
LORALEE: We agreed not to extend. We agreed to add a full wing.
LOUDON: We did. But then you demanded we add living quarters onto the studio for interview guests.
LORALEE: I tode ya I gotta have both.
LOUDON: And I told you we can't afford both. Not on top of paying for your eight-hundred-thousand-dollar tour bus.
LORALEE: That wuz last year's expense.
LOUDON: It's this year's loan.
LORALEE: I give up. I don't know what to say to ya.
LOUDON: What about, "Thank you, darling, for keeping us solvent?"
LORALEE: If I wuz in charge—
LOUDON: Don't! That sorry tune is past its expiration date.

LORALEE: People watch us becuz they wanna hear me, see me. I should have full say in how we spend—

LOUDON: Like one-point-two million for lights?

LORALEE: You have no artistic—

LOUDON: I gotta go.

LORALEE: A course you do.

(LOUDON pours coffee into a thermos.)

LORALEE: *(Pause.)* You comin' home fer lunch?

LOUDON: I'm meeting Simon and Clarice for lunch at Gino's.

LORALEE: Uh ...

(Mouth agape.)

In public? Are you outta yer damn mind?

LOUDON: Don't curse like that.

LORALEE: I'll cuss when and where I "the fuck" see fit!

LOUDON: "Fit" is an appropriate description for you.

LORALEE: I ain't havin' no fit.

LOUDON: On the verge. Be sure to take your blood pressure meds.

(He walks toward door.)

LORALEE: Don't walk out on me. This church is mine, too. I kin do what I want with it.

LOUDON: God save us all.

(Exits.)

LORALEE: *(To self.)* I don't need him. Nobody needs him.

(Opens door and yells.)

I hope you rot in hell!

(Slams door.)

(SIMON enters.)

LORALEE: Yer jest like him!

SIMON: *(Nonchalant as searches for keys.)* Like Dad? That's a relief.

LORALEE: Maybe worse.

SIMON: Did I leave my car keys in here? I thought I put them in the key basket.

LORALEE: Where *you* goin'?

SIMON: I left my favorite hat at Thorton's. I want to wear it at lunch.

LORALEE: *(Suddenly enforced calmness and sweetness.)* The red Disney World hat I bought you?

SIMON: The Duke blue hat I bought me.

LORALEE: You lose hats as fast as Daddy losin' readin' glasses.

SIMON: Dad doesn't wear reading glasses.

LORALEE: *My* daddy.

SIMON: Oh. Him.

LORALEE: Where you goin' fer lunch?

SIMON: *(Still searching.)* Uh, little dive you never heard of.

LORALEE: What its name?

SIMON: Gino's.

LORALEE: Are you kiddin' me? I love Gino's three-meat pizza!

SIMON: As much as chicken nuggets?

LORALEE: Same. Who you eatin' with?

SIMON: Oh, uh ... Dad. Clarice.

LORALEE: I'm free fer lunch.

SIMON: We're having a lengthy lunch. Planning a camping trip.

LORALEE: I hate campin'!

SIMON: Exactly.

LORALEE: Bugs. Dirt. Burnt food.

SIMON: Reasons we didn't invite you.

LORALEE: But I adore Gino's.

SIMON: Mom? You are rude to Clarice. It wouldn't be a peaceful, comfortable dining experience.

LORALEE: Hell! I kin be nice!

SIMON: Refresh my memory.

LORALEE: Children do not talk to their mamas with such, such ... ill-mannered contempt.

SIMON: Mom? Look at me. Here. Into my eyes.
(LORALEE looks.)
SIMON: *(Firmly.)* No.

LORALEE: Why must you be so difficult to raise?

SIMON: Why must *you* be so difficult to raise?
LORALEE: I'm the parent.
SIMON: I keep hoping.
   (He exits.)
LORALEE: I'm not sure I followed all'a that.
   (Yells into house.)
Clarice! You wanna come in here? Take a turn at bashin' me?
   (Speaks to self.)
I like my one-point-two million dollar lights.

(Lights to black.)

Scene Six: Phillips' Kitchen - Day

Similar to scene one, LORALEE is fastening her black bra behind her back.

LORALEE: Why can't they make these things with velcro hooks so I don't sprain my shoulder?

HOWIE: *(Yells from floor, hidden behind counter.)* I ain't finished!

LORALEE: Oh yer plum finished. You need a gallon'a milk or somethin' to git replenished.

HOWIE: *(Emerging from behind counter in boxers.)* You never leave me git satisfied.

LORALEE: Satisfyin' you would take a tribe. Git dressed. When Simon said, "a lengthy lunch," he didn't specify how lengthy.

HOWIE: *(Looks at watch.)* I wuz only down here with ya five minutes. Five ain't "lengthy."

LORALEE: Tell me 'bout it.
(Snaps fingers.)
Clothes! Now!

HOWIE: Always bossy.

LORALEE: It's my nature.

HOWIE: You probably boss God, too.

LORALEE: All day long—Hurry.

HOWIE: *(Dressing.)* Don't you never slow down?

LORALEE: When I count my money. I like listenin' to metal clankin'. Like the feel'a each piece'a paper.

HOWIE: Guess you wuz born rollin' in piles'a money.

LORALEE: When I wuz little, me and my four brothers slept in a broke-down station wagon out back. Pissed in an ole jug. Ate Cracker Jacks and jerky.

HOWIE: I thought you growed up rich. A big tobacco plantation.

LORALEE: Tenant farmers. Owner give Daddy a little scratch'a land to farm his own piddly tobacco. At least we had more than them trashy coloreds other end'a the field. But land sakes we wuz poor. I gone to bed early jest so I didn't feel hungry all night.

HOWIE: I used to do that ... So, why you act like you wuz *born* in money?

LORALEE: Only money I seen 'fore high school? Monopoly money.

HOWIE: Play money?

LORALEE: My brothers hated me always winnin'. I won big!

HOWIE: It's a game'a chance.

LORALEE: Not the way I play. Then mama left. Only come crawlin' back after I wuz growed'n married. To git hold'a my money.

(Pause.)

Howie Fitch! You are the slowest dresser'a any man on this planet!

HOWIE: You know how fast every man on this planet dresses?

LORALEE: Loudon, you. One man, one boy. Loudon changes his clothes faster'n Superman, but in bed? Slow as a limp snail. Falls asleep on top'a me.

HOWIE: I might be slow dressin', but in bed I's magic fast.

LORALEE: Like a boy. Go out the back way.

HOWIE: I ain't got my boots on yet.

(He puts on cowboy boots in silence.)

HOWIE: How come you divulged all that to me?

LORALEE: What?

HOWIE: 'Bout bein' poor, hungry. First time you ever talked to me 'bout personal mess.

LORALEE: *(Shrugs.)* Jest ... cuz.

HOWIE: You really only been with me and Reverend Phillips? Jest us two?

LORALEE: Two losers. Story'a my life.

HOWIE: Shit. Lucky life. Mercedez Benz, pool table, yer own gymnasium.

LORALEE: Kin I ask ya somethin'?

HOWIE: Guess I owe you now, don't I?

LORALEE: Is yer brother and uncle in the klan?

31

HOWIE: What?
LORALEE: The klan? You know? Ku Klux Klan—
HOWIE: I know what the klan is! No! They wudn't tell me if they wuz.
LORALEE: How come?
HOWIE: We ain't in agreement. 'Sides. We ain't on speakin' terms. Why you askin'?
LORALEE: No reason.
HOWIE: You got more reasons than I got nails and screws.
LORALEE: Jest ... I hear things. Ways klan kinda people talk.
HOWIE: 'Bout?
LORALEE: I'm a minister. People confide private affairs.
HOWIE: I ain't no dentist. I ain't gonna stand here pullin' stuff outta yer mouth all day.
LORALEE: Folks trust me to not tell.
HOWIE: Gossip.
LORALEE: You don't talk 'bout us, do ya?
HOWIE: Hell no.
LORALEE: No braggin' to the boys or—
HOWIE: No!
LORALEE: Or to girls?
HOWIE: What do you think I am?
LORALEE: I know what you are. I jest wanna know if you talk about it.
HOWIE: Screw you.
LORALEE: You jest did.
HOWIE: You think'a me like that? Me and my family'd be in the klan?
LORALEE: Klans is secret. I don't know who's in'em and who ain't.
HOWIE: *(Walking to door.)* You need help. The way you see this world? Ain't healthy.
LORALEE: I'm a minister.
HOWIE: A conivin' hypocrite. Yep. Indeed you are a minister.
LORALEE: Git out!

HOWIE: I am. And don't worry. I ain't comin' back. Have a fine Christian life, "Reverend."
(He exits.)
LORALEE: *(To self.)* I growed tired of his ways anyhow.
(She primps as dresses.)
He'll crawl back. He's male.
(Talks into fourth-wall mirror as combs hair.)
God? I done all I promised ya. Kept yer secret. Ain't tode a soul 'bout you bein' the biggest hypocrite. Creatin' all good and evil. Makin' evil delicious fun. Laughin' at us fightin' to balance it all out. Yer secret's safe. Long as yer good to me. How 'bout you show you appreciate me? Help me git my church away from Loudon. Git rid'a all these tiresome little people in my way. Tell you what, God. Make it happen soon.

(Lights to black.)

Scene Seven: Church Pulpit - Night

LORALEE stands at a spot-lit pulpit, with the audience as her congregation.

LORALEE: Thank you Dalton, honey, fer yer lovely organ music. Glided me up to this pulpit, makin' me feel light as a angel glidin' on a puffy cloud. Wudn't it beautiful, folks? Thank you, Dalton sugar. And you know what? This is the most enormous turnout anybody's ever had in this big ole sanctuary. The most big. Come to hear little me. And did you glimpse all them gorgeous white lilies linin' my path to Jesus? Thank you, Ellen. So much inspiration pourin' outta you. And Ernie! Oh my golly! Purity in yer blue lightin'! Where do you three git so much gifted ideas?—probably from me—We do live in a rich time, dudn't we folks? All cuz Lord Jesus believes in us every bit as strong as we believe in him. Wy, jest the other day, this young man come 'round my place, bless his soul, asked me if I grew up rich. Rich?! Me?! Meanin' money rich a'course, not rich in spirit. And I tode him, "Goodness gracious, honey. I growed up poor in money." I splained to that young man—boy, how when I wuz little, me and my four sufferin' brothers had to sleep on a cold, wood floor by a puny cast-iron stove. We only had logs enough fer one fire a week—Daddy built a fire every Sunday. Tode us, "On the holy day, Jesus wants yer body to be warm as yer hearts." And that boy looked at me all funny like and said, "Wy thank you, Loralee. Now Jesus is in my heart, too."Ain't that great, folks? Jest like that—
(Snaps her fingers.)
Praise the Lord. Y'all join in. Come on now. Praise the Lord.
(Laughs).

You kin do better'n that. All you souls out there watchin' on yer big-screen TVs at home join in, too now. Let me hear y'all! Praise the Lord!
(Nods and signals that was not so good but ...)
I hope it's louder'n that in yer hearts—I know it is. And now, after allowin' Jesus to love me dearly, my body is warm as my full heart is blessed every day.
(She yells.)
Praise the Lord! Hallelujah! Dalton? Wonderful choir? Kin we have another fantastic, inspiration song?

(Music plays as lights go to black.)

INTERMISSION

Scene Eight: Phillips' Living Room · Night

LORALEE enters through front door, carrying a dry-cleaned coat wrapped in plastic. LOUDON follows, carrying mail and newspaper.

LORALEE: Don't keep accusin' me'a writin' you outta deliverin' no prayer! Dalton hisself asked the choir to sing extra.
(She hangs coat in closet.)
LOUDON: He told me it was your idea.
LORALEE: Maybe it wuz. Maybe it wudn't. I got too much on my mind. You springin' house guests on me and all.
LOUDON: *Guest.* Singular. *One* guest. I didn't know Clarice's mom was going to die. I didn't know Clarice was coming to visit.
LORALEE: Un·in·vi·ted guest.
LOUDON: Sssh!
LORALEE: It's my house! Don't sssh me!
LOUDON: Fine.
(He sits and sorts mail.)
LORALEE: Where are they?
LOUDON: Who?
LORALEE: Who else would be inside'a this crowded house?
LOUDON: I wouldn't call twelve·thousand square feet "crowded." They probably went to a movie.
LORALEE: A drive·in I pray.
LOUDON: There are no drive·in theatres anymore.
LORALEE: No drive·ins? That's sad. Makes me feel old.
(She sits and pouts.)
LOUDON: You know something I enjoy about you?
LORALEE: *(Happy.)* What?
LOUDON: You can't stay mad long. You distract yourself.
(He reads newspaper.)
LORALEE: Oh.
LOUDON: Hm. Hurricane moved to the gulf. A category three.

LORALEE: *(Abruptly angry again.)* I'm still upset!
LOUDON: *(Disinterested.)* About?
LORALEE: Whatever upset me a minute ago!
LOUDON: Uh-huh.
LORALEE: *(Abruptly happy.)* Did you like my sermon tonight?
LOUDON: It ... accurately captured your heart.
LORALEE: Didn't it? I poured out every bit'a genuine love left in me.
LOUDON: The very last drop.
LORALEE: I know. Let's me and you go to a movie.
LOUDON: It's late.
LORALEE: Not tonight, silly. This week. A Debbie Reynolds' movie.
LOUDON: She died.
LORALEE: Debbie's dead?
LOUDON: Her daughter, too.
LORALEE: This world jest gits sadder and sadder. I swanee.
LOUDON: Did that Howard guy repair the coffee maker?
LORALEE: Howie. Howie Fitch.
LOUDON: Howie guy repair the—
LORALEE: Jest needed a new plug.
LOUDON: I could have attached a plug. Glad you didn't go buy a new maker.
LORALEE: I bought two of'em. Extra one fer my dressin' room. You want one fer yer's?
LOUDON: I don't drink coffee while dressing.
LORALEE: That's right, when it comes to dressin', yer magic fast.
(LORALEE is momentarily quiet, then clears her throat, trying to get attention. Eventually LOUDON looks at her.)
LOUDON: What?
LORALEE: Nothin'.
(As soon as LOUDON resumes looking at newspaper, LORALEE speaks.)

LORALEE: I heard some'a Howie's family belongs to the Ku Klux Klan.

LOUDON: *(Remains disinterested.)* Who?

LORALEE: The repair guy. His uncle and brother.

LOUDON: There aren't any klans anymore.

LORALEE: You'd be surprised.

LOUDON: If there were a klan, I would be surprised. *(Looks at newspaper.)* Drought in Oklahoma. Maybe the hurricane will help end their drought.

LORALEE: Then I guess we don't need to worry.

LOUDON: Hmm.

LORALEE: Don't want'em burnin' crosses on our new-seeded lawn.

LOUDON: *(Slams newspaper onto table.)* For gosh sakes, Loralee. Drive-ins, Debbie Reynolds, KKK. Move into this century.

LORALEE: Fer yer information? There's two drive-ins between here and Myrtle Beach. I pointed'em out to ya, but you wudn't look. Ole Debbie Reynolds' movies and Sophia Loren and Frank Sinatra and Elvis movies all play down at the Rialto. And? *And?* The klan is alive and threatenin' people all over. They jest re-branded'em selfs. Yer such a know-it-all! Don't git too comfortable! *(She exits in a huff.)*

LOUDON: *(To self.)* She's been threatening me as long as I remember. *(Pours a scotch and sips.)*

(SIMON and CLARICE enter, a bit intoxicated, laughing and being very friendly.)

SIMON: Oh! You're still up.

LOUDON: Didn't mean to surpass my bedtime and spoil your fun. Go back out, I'll retire, then you can re-enter.

SIMON: Funny, Dad.

CLARICE: *(Laughs.)* You two are so cute together!

SIMON: Cute?

LOUDON: Aging dodger and feisty whippersnapper.

SIMON: On second thought. Let's leave. Allow him to retire.

CLARICE: I don't want to leave.

SIMON: I was trying to rescue you from Dad's weather reports.

LOUDON: I never report the weather.

CLARICE: Where's Mrs. Reverend Phillips?

SIMON: Oh no, no, no. Do *not* raise her from the dead.

LORALEE: *(Yells from offstage.)* I kin hear you!

SIMON: *(Yells.)* Because you're behind the door eavesdropping!

(SIMON and CLARICE snicker.)

SIMON: *(Yells.)* How fantastic was your sermon?!

(They wait for a response that never comes.)

SIMON: She's still there listening.

CLARICE: *(Yells.)* Good night, Mrs. Reverend Phillips! Sweet dreams!

(SIMON signals, "watch this." Takes his time and then speaks loudly.)

SIMON: Oh my gosh! I'm so sorry. Mom has a terminator come every month. I've never seen a bug with so many legs.

(LORALEE rushes into room.)

LORALEE: Where?! What kinda bug? On the couch? Where? *(She realizes that all three are grinning at her.)* Y'all! Simon Alfred Phillips! That wuz cruel. God doesn't smile on such behavior. He punishes it! You will pay dearly! All three'a ya! *(She cries profusely and rushes from the room.)*

LOUDON: I knew that wasn't going to go down well. She is mortified by crawly things. You should go make peace with her.

SIMON: No way! She'd throw her purse at me.

LOUDON: More likely a heavy vase.

CLARICE: I feel terrible.
SIMON: You didn't do anything.
CLARICE: I smiled.
SIMON: True. In Mom's book, smiling is a mortal sin. Smiling earned me many knots on my head.
LOUDON: I'll go talk to her. You owe me, bud.
(He exits.)
CLARICE: She already didn't like me.
SIMON: She never liked me.
CLARICE: Right.
SIMON: It's true. She didn't want children. I was an accident.
CLARICE: I don't believe that.
SIMON: She especially didn't want a boy. She was the only girl in her family. Had to fight off four brothers.
CLARICE: Having four older brothers would be rough.
SIMON: *Younger* brothers. So, did you finally choose where we should go camping?
CLARICE: Somewhere not cold.
SIMON: Okay ... Mount Rogers. Highest peak in Virginia. Just over the line. It's summer, so, sweater weather at night, T-shirts in the day.
CLARICE: How far of a hike?
SIMON: Four, five, eight miles.
(Seductive.)
As far as you're willing to go.
CLARICE: My gear's all in Raleigh.
SIMON: I got plenty. Sleeping bags, mats, an expedition tent. Of course we can sleep in my Land Cruiser if you're scared of bears.
CLARICE: I've camped around tons of bears, Mr. Professional Solo Camper. And elk, and coyotes, and—
SIMON: That's right, Colorado lady. Were you carrying a gun?
CLARICE: No! Do you carry a gun?
SIMON: Uh, sure.

CLARICE: Wild animals are beautiful. Why would you want to shoot something so innocent?

SIMON: I hunt deer. I like eating venison.

(CLARICE quietly pouts.)

SIMON: That's right. You're a vegetarian. Tell you what. For you? I'll only shoot apples out of trees. Non-innocent apples.

(CLARICE frowns but then can't help but laugh. SIMON kisses her.)

(Lights to black.)

Scene Nine: Phillips' Kitchen - Day

LORALEE is standing at the counter. She places a sandwich into the counter-top toaster. There is a knock on the door.

LORALEE: Come in!

(HOWIE enters.)

LORALEE: Toastin' me a turkey sandwich. Want one?
HOWIE: You left a message yer toaster wuz broke.
LORALEE: And you said you wudn't comin' back.
HOWIE: I forgave you.
LORALEE: Anxious to be lovin' agin, huh?
HOWIE: Anxious to heat up yer toaster.
(He partially unbuttons his shirt.)
LORALEE: Wait! I ain't feelin' lovin' this minute.
HOWIE: I got a feelin' needs fixin' bad.
LORALEE: First things first. I need yer uncle's phone number.
HOWIE: I got eleven uncles.
LORALEE: Yer Uncle Turner.
HOWIE: *(Stops undressing and pauses.)* Fer what?
LORALEE: Oh. A little advice now and then.
HOWIE: Uncle Turner don't hand out healthy advice.
LORALEE: You got his number or not?
HOWIE: He goes to yer church. You ain't got his number?
LORALEE: A ole number. Don't belong to nobody now.
HOWIE: Try directory assistance.
LORALEE: I tried information, the internet, yer sister Charlene.
HOWIE: What'd Charlene say?
LORALEE: Soon as I spoke Turner's name, she hung up.
HOWIE: She don't go near him. Not since second grade.
LORALEE: I ain't got time to pry into family. Jest need his friggin' number.

HOWIE: I ain't got it.

LORALEE: Find it!

HOWIE: *(Pause.)* I run into his son Mason here and there. Does carpenter work on condos out at the lake.

LORALEE: Ask'im.

HOWIE: What kinda business you got with somebody no good like him?

LORALEE: Personal.

HOWIE: This gotta do with the klan?

LORALEE: Ain't you heard? There ain't klans no more. Did you know—And I'm bettin' you don't—The klan in North Carolina wuz the first police-type force in all America. Created to keep people safe.

HOWIE: I ain't askin' Mason.

LORALEE: You ain't?

(HOWIE does not respond.)

LORALEE: And I wuz jest startin' to feel lovin' fer ya. Hot and lovin'.

(She unbuttons HOWIE'S' shirt.)

LORALEE: What? You ain't feelin hot fer me now, baby doll?

(HOWIE pushes her away and buttons his shirt.)

LORALEE: Well now. That sure is one-big shame.

HOWIE: Yer toaster looks to be workin' fine.

(HOWIE walks toward door.)

LORALEE: Guess I'll set here all lonely like. Rewrite my sermon.

HOWIE: Do that.

LORALEE: 'Bout you.

HOWIE: *(Stops.)* What?

LORALEE: I ain't personally honored nobody from my great big congregation in a long, long time. Groups'a people, yep. But not singled out somebody *special* fer recognition.

HOWIE: What'cha gonna say 'bout me?

LORALEE: I wuz thinkin' 'bout maybe ... a story. Story 'bout a young man—no name a course—young man stealin' from a little car repair shop where he used to pick up ... *extra* cash.

HOWIE: I paid'em back in full. Two year ago.

LORALEE: That's right. You *sneaked* money out. You *sneaked* money back in. Hopin' they'd never know. That little car repair shop accused the wrong boy. Rudy, right? Rudy. Nobody'd hire poor Rudy agin. Caused his girlfriend to up and leave him. Run off with their baby. Must'a hurt awful. Enough he killt hisself. Eighteen years old ... Dead.

(HOWIE slowly kneels, trembling.)

LORALEE: I love me stories that sends a strong message. Needs a bit'a spicin' up. I know! I'll add how that boy— the boy who took the money, not the boy who shot his brains out—how that sinner boy—the one who committed thievery—turned his life plum 'round. Found God. That'll move folks in my church. Folks watchin' me on TV. Heck! It'll help sinners 'round the world. You like my story?

HOWIE: Everybody'll know it's me.

LORALEE: Honey? Kin you git yer uncle's number from Mason?

HOWIE: *(Pauses to plan.)* Maybe I'll tell people 'bout me and you sinnin'.

LORALEE: You could. Yep. A course, my sermon's tonight. It'd look like you gone crazy. Made up tall tales to git even. I'll tell folks I feel sorry fer ya. You fall'in from grace agin.

HOWIE: *(Long pause.)* Uncle Turner's number's on my phone. Mama's stayin' out at his place. Tryin' to kick her oxy pills.

LORALEE: Well, praise the Lord! He does work in mysterious ways. Don't he now?

(Lights to black.)

Scene Ten: Phillips' Living Room - Day

LORALEE, sitting on the couch, is anxious and plotting. CLARICE and SIMON enter from inside of the house and walk toward the front door.

LORALEE: Where you two headed?
CLARICE: I'm shopping for some new hiking boots.
LORALEE: Hikin'?
SIMON: Walking shoes.
CLARICE: Walking. All I brought from home were sandals. I'm getting blisters.
SIMON: Later, Mom.
CLARICE: Bye, Mrs. Phillips. Uh, Reverend.
(CLARICE and SIMON exit. LORALEE walks to the window to make certain they are gone, and then darts back into the house. She emerges with the small orange package. She examines it, and then cautiously uses a letter opener to detach the tape. She pulls out a framed photo and stares at it.)
LORALEE: Ah. Loudon when he wuz little. How precious. Wonder who that other boy is.

(CLARICE re-enters and LORALEE hides the photo.)

CLARICE: Forgot my wallet.
(She exits back into the house and LORALEE re-tapes the wrapping paper.)

(CLARICE returns and again LORALEE hides package.)

CLARICE: Found it. Have a nice afternoon.
LORALEE: Clarice, honey?
CLARICE: Yes ma'am?
LORALEE: Did you ever give the Reverend that package you brung with you?
CLARICE: Package?
LORALEE: Little orange one?

CLARICE: Oh! No. Thank you for reminding me.
(She walks toward front door.)
LORALEE: I'm highly curious—You know how I am. What gift did yer mama send Loudon?
CLARICE: Some old photo. I forget what she said it was. School or sports something.
LORALEE: Loudon by hisself?
CLARICE: I never saw it. Simon's waiting. Sorry to rush off.
LORALEE: No, no, honey bunch. That's fine. You two be careful now.
(CLARICE exits.)
LORALEE: *(Re-opens package and stares.)* Not high school. He ain't even got his Adam's apple ... Pier out at the lake. Drippin' wet. Sure wore skimpy suits back then. Arms 'round each other's shoulders ... Middle school maybe.
(She suddenly hurries to bookshelves, gets down on knees and reads from bindings on books on bottom shelf.)
"High school, high school, Albemarle Middle."
(She pulls book from shelf and looks at index pages.)
"M."
(Turns page.)
"O. P ... Phillips. Pages 78 and 93."
(Turns pages.)
"75, 78 ... Loudon Ralston Phillips" ... Huh. Braces. Awfully homely back then.
(Turns pages.)
Page 93 ... 93 ... "Debate team." Figures. Cuter in that pic. Like the swimmin' pic.
(Pauses, then turns to index and searches.)
Rs ... Ts ... "Tennyson ... Thomas ... Thompkins ... Alex Thompkins. Chris Thompkins. Page 80."
(She searches for page, then photo.)
"Sommers ... Thom, Thom ... Thompkins!"
(Pauses, confused.)

"Chris ... Thompkins" ... A boy. No Chris Ann. Let me look agin.
(Looks at index.)
"Alex. Chris" ... No Chris Ann.
(Returns to photo page.)
Chris ... No Chris Ann ... Same boy in swim photo ... Friends.
(She places both hands over mouth, dumbstruck.)

(LOUDON enters from inside house and LORALEE screams.)

LOUDON: Sorry, sorry.
(He laughs.)
Didn't mean to scare you. I parked out back.
LORALEE: Oh my heart. I almost peed on myself.
(She holds her chest. Struggles to catch her breath.)
LOUDON: You okay?
LORALEE: Fine, fine. Jest lookin' fer a dictionary.
LOUDON: Those are yearbooks. One shelf up. I haven't used a dictionary in years. Internet's faster.
LORALEE: My phone wuz in the bedroom.
LOUDON: What's that? A gift?
LORALEE: This? Nothin'. Dalton dropped it off. Little gift book fer me to sign fer his niece. She watches our show.
LOUDON: Want me to sign it?
LORALEE: No. I almost got it wrapped.
LOUDON: Orange? I need a clean shirt. Splattered coffee on this one.
(Yells as he exits into house.)
Supposed to rain again tonight.
(LORALEE slides the yearbook into place and pours a gin drink.)
LORALEE: A boy ... Chris ... How could that boy grow up to be somebody's mama?
(Pause.)
Friends.

(She is unable to drink and cries for a short moment, and then forces composure. Speaks to self.)
God? You even there? I'm gonna git through this. Climb up top. I'll show ya.
(Gulps drink.)

(Lights to black.)

Scene Eleven: Phillips' Living Room - Night

SIMON is performing sit-ups on the floor. Sound of doorbell.

SIMON: Really?!
(He answers door.)
HOWIE: Okay if I come in?
SIMON: Mom's not here.
HOWIE: I know. They's preachin' on TV.
SIMON: *(Awkward pause.)* How are you?
HOWIE: Okay. How you?

(CLARICE, wearing boots, enters from inside house.)

CLARICE: These are way too big.
SIMON: Wear thick hiking socks.
CLARICE: Oh. Sorry. Didn't know you had company.
HOWIE: I ain't company.
SIMON: Clarice? This is Howie. Howie? This is Clarice.
CLARICE: Nice to meet you, Howie.
HOWIE: You too, ma'am.
CLARICE: Ma'am?
(Laughs.)
No one's ever addressed me as, "ma'am."
HOWIE: *(Embarrassed.)* Sorry. I jest ... jest—
CLARICE: No, no. That's fine. Kind of cute.
SIMON: Come in. Can I get you something? Water? Tea?
HOWIE: I need to tell ya somethin' important.
(Awkward pause.)
CLARICE: Oh! Sorry. I'll leave you two alone. Grab my *thick* hiking socks.
(She exits.)
SIMON: Have a seat.
HOWIE: I kin stand.
SIMON: Oh ... Okay.
(They both remain standing.)
SIMON: What's up?

49

HOWIE: Yer mother.
SIMON: She didn't pay you? Damn it! She forgets half the time. Hurts people's feelings right and left. Sorry.
HOWIE: No! Not that. She paid me. Amply.
SIMON: Amply?
(Chuckles.)
Unusual for my mom. Stingy as—
HOWIE: I come to warn ya.
SIMON: Warn me?
HOWIE: 'Bout yer mother.
SIMON: Oh! You don't need to warn me about her. I know all about—
HOWIE: She's dangerous—
SIMON: Tell me about it. She—
HOWIE: Serious.
SIMON: *(Pauses as becomes concerned.)* What's she done?
HOWIE: Asked fer my uncle's number.
SIMON: For?
HOWIE: He uh ... cuz . . .
SIMON: Yeah?
HOWIE: I . . .
(He shuts down.)
SIMON: Your uncle in the klan?
(HOWIE nods and they both remain silent for a moment.)
SIMON: Did she say why?
HOWIE: *(Shrugs.)* Advice.
SIMON: About?
(HOWIE shrugs and shakes head.)
SIMON: Damn!
HOWIE: I better go.
SIMON: No! ... Thank you, Howie. I ... I've never been nice to you. I apologize. I feel really bad about that.
(HOWIE nods with embarrassment. SIMON extends his hand. Eventually, HOWIE shakes hand and exits.)
SIMON: *(Yells.)* Clarice?

(CLARICE enters.)

CLARICE: Thick socks did the trick. Where's Howie?
SIMON: We've got problems. My mom.
CLARICE: I told you she hates me.
SIMON: We need to speed up our camping plans.

(Lights to black.)

Scene Twelve: Phillips' Living Room - Night

LOUDON is reading the newspaper. LORALEE, holding a note, storms in from the bedrooms.

LORALEE: Look at this!
(LOUDON reads beginning of note and shrugs.)
LOUDON: They went camping. Good. Clear, warm weather all weekend.
LORALEE: Read the rest'a it!
(LOUDON reads more.)
LORALEE: Not comin' back!
LOUDON: What argument did you two have?
LORALEE: *She* put'im up to this.
LOUDON: Clarice?
LORALEE: She kidnapped him!
LOUDON: Oh, for gosh sakes. Did they take Buster?
LORALEE: I ain't heard no barkin'!
LOUDON: Simon always takes Buster camping, always brings him home. He knows that dog is getting old and set in his ways.
LORALEE: Where'd they go?
LOUDON: Probably down by the creek near the golf course.
LORALEE: He tode me they wuz plannin' a big trip.
LOUDON: Not until after baseball season.
LORALEE: Where wuz it to? The big trip?
LOUDON: Uh ... Mount Rogers.
LORALEE: Where the heck is that?
LOUDON: Up through Roaring Gap, past Mouth of Wilson, Virginia.
LORALEE: Virginia?!
LOUDON: Just three-hours.
LORALEE: She kidnapped him!
LOUDON: No one kidnapped anyone. Stop saying that.
LORALEE: She's in college. He's a high school junior.
LOUDON: Senior.
LORALEE: Are you gonna do somethin'?

LOUDON: Go look for them? They'll be home before I get out of the driveway.

LORALEE: So! Yer not gonna help.

LOUDON: There's nothing to help.

LORALEE: Fine. I know somebody who will help me.

LOUDON: Who? Simon's baseball team? Form a search party?

LORALEE: Oh. You think this is some kinda joke.

LOUDON: We both have tonight off.

(Stands.)

Let me take you to dinner.

LORALEE: Don't sweet talk me! This is yer fault!

LOUDON: What? I worked a love spell on them?

LORALEE: They better not be in love. I didn't raise Simon to be like that.

LOUDON: Not to be friendly, loving? And pardon me, I believe *we* raised him. Not you alone.

LORALEE: You poisoned him!

LOUDON: Take some slow, deep breaths and—

LORALEE: Fuck you!

(LOUDON steps back and gestures he's backing off.)

LORALEE: I know about you. Yer sick!

(LOUDON doesn't know what to do for a moment.)

LOUDON: Let me grab us a couple of beers.

LORALEE: I don't want yer filthy beers, yer filthy liquor. Yer always try to git me sinnin'. No more drinkin! No more sex! No more lettin' you poison our son!

LOUDON: How the heck do I poison Simon?!

LORALEE: You know.

LOUDON: For the life of me I don't.

LORALEE: Uh huh. Bet that trashy girl knows, too.

LOUDON: Knows what?!

LORALEE: 'Bout her mama.

LOUDON: Chris Ann?

(LORALEE walks to shelf and unwraps orange paper from photo.)

LORALEE: There weren't no Chris Ann. Never wuz. Not in yer elementary school. Not in yer middle school, high school.

LOUDON: I didn't know Chris Ann in school. I told you.

LORALEE: Right. Right. Uh huh. But you knew ... Chris.

LOUDON: *(Taken aback.)* What?

LORALEE: Chris and Alex.

LOUDON: What are you talking about?

LORALEE: Chris and Alex Thompkins. Brothers.

(LOUDON is speechless.)

LORALEE: Uh huh. Brothers. Boys. Two boys. Care to 'splain this?

(LORALEE shoves photo in front of LOUDON, who stares at it.)

LORALEE: Didn't think so. I figured it out. That boy Chris grew up. Become Chris Ann.

LOUDON: She ... I mean he—

LORALEE: Confusin', ain't it? Poison!

LOUDON: It's not what ... how you see it.

LORALEE: Oh! Tell me. This is pure fascinatin'.

LOUDON: Chris always knew. From kindergarten on. Even before. She knew—

LORALEE: He!

LOUDON: *(Pauses, calm.)* No. Not he. She.

LORALEE: Poison!

LOUDON: Not poison. Truth.

LORALEE: *(Laughs.)* Truth? You call changin ' yer sex— that crap—"truth?" Fine. I'm an alien. Flew here from Jupiter. Disguised myself. Fooled you into marryin' me. Both our kids? Half aliens.

LOUDON: There's no reason to mock Chris Ann. You are being mean and ridiculous.

LORALEE: I'm ridiculous?

LOUDON: Yes.

LORALEE: Did you sleep with him? Her? Him her. Hell! I don't what to call it.

(LOUDON stares at floor.)

LORALEE: *(Screams.)* Did ya?!
LOUDON: In middle school we—
LORALEE: I want you outta here!
LOUDON: Nothin' but—
LORALEE: Did you hear me?!
LOUDON: You aren't listening.
LORALEE: I'm through listenin'! You pack that fancy Gucci leather suitcase'a yers and git! You got that?
LOUDON: This is my house.
LORALEE: Ain't no more. And that church ain't yers neither! Not no more! Not 'less you want me informin' everybody how you slept with a boy who changed hisself into a woman, who probably used woman bathrooms. Did he? Preyin' on little girls and old ladies in bathrooms?!
LOUDON: Chris was one of the most decent people ever born on this planet—
LORALEE: Decent?! Yer so messed up you ain't got none'a that "moral compass" left you love preachin' 'bout. You know what I done all afternoon?
(LOUDON shakes his head.)
LORALEE: Writ my sermon. Asked forgiveness fer yer and Chris's souls. One'a my best. Only thin' that'll stop me from deliverin' my juicy, powerful sermon is—

(LOUDON leaps up and slaps LORALEE.)

LORALEE: *(Pausing to recover.)* Well now ... You been achin' to do that a long time. Showed all over yer face. You hate me. Now I know why.
(LOUDON stares at her with a clinched fist.)
LORALEE: I'm a woman. Not a man-woman like you fancy. Jest a plain, simple woman.
(She chuckles.)
Now we kin add wife abuse to all that bad in you. I got calls to make. If I wuz you? I'd pack and git as far off as I kin.

(LOUDON collapses.)

LORALEE: Oh. And like I tode ya before. Don't git too comfortable. What you deserve is comin' yer way. *(She exits.)*

(LOUDON looks at photo and then breaks down crying.)

(Lights to black.)

Scene Thirteen: Loralee in spotlight - Night

LORALEE, sitting in a spot-lit chair, calls from a phone on a night table.

LORALEE: Mr. Turner Fitch? Hi. This is Reverend Loralee Phillips. Wy how are you this fine evening? ... Thank ya fer askin'. I couldn't be better. I ain't seen you in church in the longest time. I hope you ain't abandoned us ... Well, I am so relieved to hear that. You had me worried somethin' awful. Listen. I got a tiny problem and wuz wonderin' if you had advice fer me. I gotta woman in our congregation who begged me fer help.
(Pause.)
Well—and this is between you and I—Her son wuz kidnapped ... Yes sir! Her teenage baby boy kidnapped by a growed college adult woman. Drove'im across state lines. She's colored and the boy's white—I know that don't matter to ya, but ... To Virginia. Why? Does which state make a difference? ... I did not know that.
(Pause.)
So, by law the woman's an adult cuz she's over eighteen and the little boy's a minor? ... Punishable felony? You are jest gigantic help. Yer entire family line has been amazin' help to me like you would not believe. Now, should I be the one to call the police or kin you ... You are amazin' Mr. Fitch. Amazin'!

(Lights to black.)

Scene Fourteen: Camping site - Night

SIMON and CLARICE are sitting by a fire at night.

CLARICE: You look cold.
SIMON: No. Fine.
CLARICE: You're shivering.
SIMON: My clothes got wet from sweating.
CLARICE: Wrap up with this towel. It's dry.
(She gently places towel over SIMON'S shoulders, rubs his shoulders, and then looks at sky.)
Can you point out Polaris? The North Star?
SIMON: For real? I was an Eagle Scout. There. Tip of the Little Dipper.
CLARICE: Excellent.
SIMON: Now. Can you point out Beta Centauri?
(CLARICE looks at sky, twisting as she searches.)
CLARICE: Uh ... hmm ... maybe ... no ... or uh . . .
SIMON: *(Laughs.)* You can only see it from the southern hemisphere.
CLARICE: That's mean.
SIMON: I'm sorry.
CLARICE: Have you ever seen it?
SIMON: Santiago, Chile.
CLARICE: Santi—And you gave me a hard time for camping in Colorado?
SIMON: I didn't camp in Chile.
CLARICE: You went there!
SIMON: Church trip. Building housing for earthquake victims.
CLARICE: What a nice thing to do. Did your entire family go?
SIMON: My dad and I. My little sister had just started getting sick, so Mom stayed behind to watch after her.
CLARICE: I didn't know you have a sister. I haven't seen any—
SIMON: Leukemia.

CLARICE: Oh ... I'm sorry.
SIMON: Yeah ... Do you have brothers or sisters?
CLARICE: Just me.
(*SIMON nods, not able to talk more. CLARICE tries to fill in silence.*)
CLARICE: No other brothers or sisters? Older?
(*SIMON shakes head.*)
CLARICE: But two parents.
(*SIMON nods.*)
CLARICE: (*Pause.*) I had one. One parent.
SIMON: (*Mumbles.*) One.
CLARICE: That I knew. She was incredible—different, but outstanding. Other kids, families, made fun of us.
SIMON: Why?
CLARICE: She was uh ... unusual.
SIMON: How?
CLARICE: Just ... tall—for one thing. Uh, white ... I wasn't. Uh, outgoing. Confident. Stubborn. Very loving. In her own, special way.
SIMON: I wish I could have met her.
CLARICE: She would like you—love you. She lived to make life better for ... people feeling neglected or tormented. Outcasts. Lonely people.
SIMON: How did my dad fit in?
CLARICE: Uh ... Like an uncle. Sometimes, I used to pretend he was my father. A father who was away lots. Working in other countries. Not home much. Silly, huh?
SIMON: I wish you and I could have grown up sharing Dad. Your mom instead of mine.
CLARICE: Ugh!
SIMON: What?
CLARICE: Then you and I would be like brother and sister.
SIMON: You'd be a great sis.
CLARICE: Hello? I love you—I mean like.
SIMON: Oh, oh, oh. Yeah. Never mind. Not like a sister.
CLARICE: Thank you.
SIMON: Close call.

(They both break out laughing. Then they hear something making noise in the forest. They are startled and become abruptly quiet.)
CLARICE: *(Whispers.)* What was that?
SIMON: A bear ... A gigantic den of bears.
(CLARICE playfully slaps SIMON'S shoulder.)
CLARICE: Stop it.
SIMON: Okay. Only one black bear. Or an elk. Actually, probably a Rocky Mountain coyote.
CLARICE: You are such a jerk to me.
SIMON: You love it.
(CLARICE becomes silent and stares at SIMON.)
SIMON: What?
CLARICE: I do.
SIMON: Do what?
CLARICE: Love it.
(They stare at one another and then kiss. Suddenly, CLARICE pulls away.)
CLARICE: *(Whispers.)* I heard it again.
SIMON: Wind. Acorns falling.
CLARICE: No. Voices. One voice. Listen
(They are quiet for a moment.)
SIMON: I only hear your heart pounding.
CLARICE: Someone's out there.
SIMON: Nobody's out—
CLARICE: There's a light.
SIMON: I see it.
CLARICE: A flashlight.
SIMON: Yeah ... Now it's gone.
(Pauses, and then yells.)
Hey! Who's out there?
(They sit motionlessly, listening.)
CLARICE: There it is again.
SIMON: *(Yells.)* Who's there?!
CLARICE: They turned it back off.
(SIMON unrolls a piece of canvas.)
CLARICE: What are you doing?

SIMON: Getting my rifle.
CLARICE: Don't do that.
SIMON: We have no idea who's out there. What they want.
(He loads shells into the rifle, cocks it, and points it toward the woods. CLARICE moves closer to SIMON and they both sit motionlessly.)

(Lights to black.)

Scene Fifteen: Living Room - Day

LORALEE is sitting alone, dressed in her housecoat, staring at nothing. The doorbell rings once and she is unfazed. There are several knocks on the door, and she remains unfazed. The doorbell rings again and she jumps, startled from her trance. She slowly moves toward the front door, making sure her housecoat is buttoned. Before she arrives at the door, LOUDON partially opens the door and pulls a key out of the lock. He stops when he sees LORALEE.

LOUDON: Oh. I thought no one was home

LORALEE: *(Dull monotone.)* You still have yer key.

LOUDON: I can come back later if—

LORALEE: No. Yer inside.

> *(She returns to couch and sits. After an awkward moment, LOUDON fully enters.)*

LOUDON: I need to grab a few things. Just be a minute.

> *(LORALEE does not respond. LOUDON walks toward door to bedrooms and stops.)*

LOUDON: It's three o'clock. You aren't dressed.

> *(LORALEE does not respond.)*

LOUDON: Mom called today. She sent her regards.

> *(LORALEE barely nods.)*

LOUDON: They're heading to Scottsdale for a golf holiday.

> *(Pauses.)*

Mom commented you looked very elegant at the funeral.

LORALEE: She did, too.

> *(Awkward silence.)*

LOUDON: I fly out in the morning. Atlanta. Eighteen-hours to Johannesburg. A day there. Then, I don't know. Two hours, three to Zimbabwe. Then a mission bus will pick me up. Another hour or two ride. Frederick's supposed to meet me, but communications have been spotty.

LORALEE: *(Monotone.)* Who?

LOUDON: Frederick. You two met at the international fair. He's stationed in Zimbabwe.

LORALEE: Oh.
LOUDON: Can I get you anything?
LORALEE: Uh ... No.
LOUDON: I attended Clarice's memorial in Raleigh.
(No response from LORALEE.)
LOUDON: Twenty or so students. Couple of professors.
LORALEE: Oh.
LOUDON: No family, of course.
LORALEE: You.
LOUDON: Well ... I wasn't really family. Kind of ... Are you getting out of the house any? Going to the church?
(LORALEE shakes head.)
LOUDON: People are worried about you. Rayvon's doing the telecasts.
LORALEE: *(Mumbles.)* Rayvon.
LOUDON: Terribly of course.
(No response from LORALEE.)
LOUDON: Did you see the news this morning? The police officers who shot them—
LORALEE: Murdered—
LOUDON: Mur—
(Pause.)
The two officers were permanently dismissed, fired.
LORALEE: No charges?
LOUDON: Self-defense plea. Said they yelled, asked if the kids were armed. Both testified the woman yelled back that they had a rifle.
LORALEE: You give Simon that rifle.
LOUDON: He loves hunting.
LORALEE: Loved.
LOUDON: Loved ... Rayvon's willing to take care of Buster. Unless of course you changed your mind.
LORALEE: An ole half-deaf dog?
LOUDON: Yeah, well ... Clarice's classmates are organizing a protest.
LORALEE: Wave their signs fer TV cameras. At least Simon's classmates is respectful.
LOUDON: *(Pause.)* I should grab my—

LORALEE: What are you takin'?

LOUDON: My family Bible and my—

LORALEE: That's *our* family Bible.

LOUDON: The one my grandmother passed onto me after she—

LORALEE: Oh. That one. Take it.

LOUDON: I've never understood the police hiking up that trail at night.

LORALEE: Park rangers I reckon.

LOUDON: No. Police. The sheriff claimed they were having problems with locals growing marijuana in the park.

LORALEE: There you go.

LOUDON: That isn't their jurisdiction. I'm thinking about hiring an investigator to go up there and—

LORALEE: Let it go.

LOUDON: *(Taken aback.)* What did you say?

LORALEE: You have yer mission in Zimbabwe. There's nothin' left fer you here. I seen to it.

(LOUDON stares with daggers in his eyes, clinches his fists, and then exits into bedrooms. LORALEE walks to mirror, looks at self, and puts on lipstick.

(LOUDON re-enters, furious, carrying family Bible.)

LOUDON: What the hell! Simon's room's empty!

LORALEE: I donated his junk to the church rummage sale.

LOUDON: You're sick!

LORALEE: You didn't care 'bout honorin' our daughter's grave. But when yer son—

LOUDON: Evil!

LORALEE: It's called, "grievin'." You always preach to our grievin' church members, "Donate yer deceased loved one's belongin's to help you—"

LOUDON: Not after two weeks!

LORALEE: Exactly what wuz you plannin' to steal from *my* house?

LOUDON: God damn you!

LORALEE: You watch yer mouth in my home!

LOUDON: I wanted that photo of Simon and me in Santiago.

LORALEE: Oh. The one by the house you two pretended you built?

LOUDON: A team of us built it! You gave away our photo? *(He groans, grabs his chest, falls to his knees, then slumps, gasping for air.)* I can't breathe!

LORALEE: Oh my God! Don't you die on me! Loosen this! *(She loosens LOUDON'S tie.)*

LORALEE: I'll git ya some water. *(She rushes to bar and gets glass.)* Here. Drink this. *(LOUDON drinks, coughs, and spits out drink. LORALEE smells glass.)*

LORALEE: Oh gosh! That's my gin! I swear I thought it wuz water. *(She rushes to get water.)*

LOUDON: *(Gasping.)* You trying to hurry my dying?

LORALEE: I don't want'cha to die. I jest want ya to suffer eternally.

LOUDON: I'm suffering eternally.

LORALEE: Here. Sip this. *(LOUDON sips.)*

LORALEE: Better?

LOUDON: Thank you.

LORALEE: Drink more. You scared me to death, you idiot!

LOUDON: *(Crying.)* You gave away all Simon's stuff.

LORALEE: No, no. It's all down in our basement.

LOUDON: Not the rummage sale?

LORALEE: Every bit'a his stuff's downstairs. Seein' all his things kept tearin' up my heart. He wuz my baby boy. *(She cries hard. They both hug on the floor as they cry. Eventually, LORALEE sits up.)*

LORALEE: We're grieving, ain't we? Together.

LOUDON: Yep. We are.

LORALEE: Don't git too comfortable 'bout it.

LOUDON: So you told me. First time we met. Every day since.

LORALEE: I told you that?

LOUDON: Durham. Ninth Street Bar. You walked over to my table to take my beer order.

LORALEE: You wudn't old enough to drink.

LOUDON: You said you'd let it slide that one time, "But don't—

LORALEE: "Git too comfortable."

LOUDON: I never have.

LORALEE: Why'chu marry me?

LOUDON: You were the prettiest, strongest willed person I'd ever met.

LORALEE: Did you *love* me?

LOUDON: I *adored* you.

LORALEE: What changed? What'd I do wrong?

LOUDON: You have hate. For so many people.

LORALEE: I can't help I hate.

LOUDON: I know.

LORALEE: I don't know where it comes from.

LOUDON: I know you don't.

LORALEE: I kin try harder.

LOUDON: I've seen you try.

(LORALEE walks across room.)

LORALEE: Why did Simon spite our church so much?

LOUDON: He said ... he feared where it was headed.

LORALEE: Did you fear where we wuz headed?

LOUDON: I'm on my way to Zimbabwe. New beginnings. New directions.

LORALEE: Africa's far off.

LOUDON: I need far off.

LORALEE: You hanged onto me this long time. Honest truth. Why?

LOUDON: Honest truth?

(LORALEE nods and LOUDON stands.)

LOUDON: Teresa and Simon.

(LORALEE turns her back on LOUDON.)

LORALEE: I ain't gonna watch you go. I ain't gonna watch more family leave me.

(LOUDON nods, gets his Bible, and quietly exits through the front door.)

LORALEE: *(After a moment, she walks to the phone and calls.)* Angel? Tell Rayvon to move over. I'm comin' back.

(Lights to black.)

Scene Sixteen: Living Room – Day

LORALEE is primping in the mirror while talking on phone.

LORALEE: *(On phone.)* No, no, no, Harold. I don't want no organ tryin' to sound like a trumpet. I want a real trumpet! Kin you do that? I sure hope so cuz you come with only mediocre recs and outta the goodness'a my heart I took a chance on ya.

(HOWIE enters and LORALEE jumps and screams.)

LORALEE: *(Into phone.)* Nothin'. An ole friend surprised me's all. I'll call ya back. Now find me that trumpet. Hear?
(Ends call.)
What in tarnation are you doin' here? How'd'chu git in?
HOWIE: The garage code.
LORALEE: I never give you no garage code.
HOWIE: First time me and you got down.
LORALEE: Well, I must'a been outta my mind.
HOWIE: Like every time we got down.
LORALEE: This ain't a good moment fer—
HOWIE: You ain't got nobody livin' here no more.
(Walks closer to Loralee.)
LORALEE: Maybe I do, maybe I don't. What'da'ya want?
HOWIE: Jest see how yer doin'.
LORALEE: Fine. Better'n fine.
HOWIE: Good, good.
LORALEE: What about you?
HOWIE: Workin' on beach houses. Hilton Head. Pays good. Better'n good.
LORALEE: Well, ain't that wonderful!
HOWIE: I know what you did.
LORALEE: What are you talkin' about?
HOWIE: Callin' the police. Up in Virginia.
LORALEE: Yer talkin' nonsense, Howie Fitch.

HOWIE: You called my Uncle Turner.

LORALEE: I call many'a my parishioners. It's what reverends do.

HOWIE: Then you called the police.

LORALEE: I never called no Virginia police. I don't like yer unkind insinuation. I believe it's time you go.

(HOWIE moves closer.)

LORALEE: *(Backing up.)* I installed surveillance cameras all over this house. Includin' this room.

HOWIE: Too bad ya didn't have cameras before. We could'a won ourselfs home video contests.

(He holds hand up as if going to stroke her hair like old times.)

LORALEE: *(Steps back.)* Please. I don't wanna be touched.

HOWIE: *(Withdraws hand.)* Yer worried I'll hurt ya.

LORALEE: I don't know what you and yer people are capable of.

HOWIE: Jest cuz you hurt people don't mean I would. Oh, that's right. You git other people to do it fer ya.

LORALEE: Yer scarin' me.

HOWIE: *(Steps closer.)* I wuz thinkin' 'bout writin' me a sermon. Somethin' personal. Single out someone special.

LORALEE: You ain't got talent to write no sermon.

HOWIE: You sure 'bout that? A lady of grace hatin' black people. Hating'em enough to call people in the klan fer advice, all the while spewin' sweet soundin' words from the pulpit. I think people'd be plum fascinated 'bout what I got to offer.

LORALEE: I kin talk, too.

HOWIE: And *damn* yer good at it! You lie, and lie more, 'til you lie so much you believe it yerself. I seen it.

LORALEE: Jest cuz people fear lookin' at dirt I dig up don't make it not true.

HOWIE: Yer in falsehoods so deep there's no bottom. Sad Reverend Loralee Phillips. Self proclaimed. Not even really ordained, are ya? One more big ole lie.

LORALEE: *(Frightened, soft.)* Please ... Leave me alone.

HOWIE: I ain't ready to go.

LORALEE: *(Pushing HOWIE away.)* I'm callin' the police.

HOWIE: I would love to hear you explain to the police. Publish it front page.

LORALEE: What'da'ya want? Money? I'll give ya money to go away. Enough fer the rest'a yer life.

HOWIE: Money? Oh wow!

(Chuckles.)

I don't want yer money. I jest wanted to look at yer purty face. Cuz no matter what comes outta that mouth'a yers, truth is writ all over yer face. I got what I come fer.

(He walks toward front door.)

LORALEE: What are ya goin' to do?

HOWIE: Me? Uh ... Leave. Be at peace 'bout what's happenin'.

LORALEE: What's happenin'?

HOWIE: Well now ... I git to wake up every morning. Look at myself in my mirror. Knowin' at the same time,
(Pause.)
Yer lookin' at yerself in yer mirror.

(HOWIE exits through the front door. LORALEE looks in the mirror, becomes frightened of what she sees, and screams, followed by crying.)

(Loud chorus music plays during the moment of darkness between scenes.)

Scene Seventeen: Church Pulpit - Day

LORALEE walks to the spot-lit pulpit. The music stops. She speaks to the choir behind her.

LORALEE: Bless you. Bless you, choir. Lovely, lovely music. *(She turns to the audience, her congregation.)* I wanna thank all you. Yer flowers. Yer cakes, cards. Most'a all ... yer prayers ... Simon ... The light'a my life ... Took ... Like my baby girl, Teresa ... Took. But I still got what mattered to both my angel children. What they loved most. This church. They wuz sacrificed ... to bring us all together here.
(She sniffles and appears to wipe away tears, but there are none.)
This church. Our lastin' friend. Family don't last. In a flash, children can be took. Parents can be took. Love disappears. Like mornin' fog, beautiful for a moment.
(Pause.)
Gone.
(Pauses to compose.)
God! ... God turned his back on us fer a bit. Left us on our own. Commanded me to lead. And so I obeyed. This church? It may git burnt down. Git flooded. Bombed. But we rise it from dust and ashes. We build it back stronger so when God returns, he is pleased.
(Pauses to become stronger.)
What's a country? Hm? Somethin' made up by old men writin' on papers? Standin' on man-made thrones and declarin', "All this belongs to me!" No! It don't! You! Mr. so-called president. You! Mr. fake king. You! Mr. self-proclaimed ruler. *You* belong to this church. You jest ain't bright enough to know it. Startin' *now*, no police force no army no politicians no protesters no accusers no false-prophet religions kin stop us. They got guns— We sure as heck got guns. But they ain't on the right side. We *fight* fer the right side!
(Calms congregation.)

71

This mega-church y'all's sittin' in? It's our model. We's diggin' foundations fer more mega-churches. Seventeen! My sweet husband Loudon? Over workin' his butt—excuse my honest language—workin' his tail off in Africa. He don't know it, but he's standin' on land fer our first overseas mega-church. It's gonna leap up under his feet 'fore he kin say, "Hold on there, Loralee honey. Slow down, girl!" I ain't slowin' fer Loudon. I ain't slowin' fer Africa. I sure ain't slowin' fer no government. Y'all with me? ... I said y'all with me?!
(Pauses, acting as if congregation is going crazy, gesturing for them to quieten.)
Calm yer britches now.
(Turns to look at choir and then back to congregation.)
Y'all remember Rodney? Assistant manager? Gone. I asked Rodney to do what wuz needed. Tode me, "No." Don't nobody tell me "no" when it's what the church demands. What did wimpy, little, non-believer Rodney refuse to do? Put our church flag on top. Simple thing "No flag'a no nation flies higher than *the church* flag! Period!"
(Calms. Speaks softly.)
Now. Somethin' else. My communications assistant informed me, tonight we got the biggest number'a people sittin' in this church and watchin' on TV ever assembled in all history. Watchin' me. Little me from Raven, North Carolina.
(Mumbles to self.)
Come far.
(Pauses to walk away and then back to pulpit.)
Tomorrow? I want all'a y'all, to join celebratin'. The most enormous church ceremony. Bigger'n Billy Graham, Oral Roberts, the popes, all of'em added up together. We gonna raise the church flag to its rightful place. Above *all* flags!
(Gestures for congregation to calm.)

Ellen? I want ya to line all them aisles in here with white lilies. So, when these fine folks walk in tomorrow night, they kin feel what I feel. Glidin'. Glidin' on puffy clouds. Like angels.
(Giggles like a school kid.)
I am so bubblin' over with joy. Love. Spreadin' it, sharin' fast as I kin.
(Points to organist.)
Harold? He's our new organist—Dalton wuz slow—Harold? I feel like a beautiful hymn. Play me, sing me—
(Pauses to reflect.)
Somethin' with a God-pleasin', real trumpet call.
(Turns to congregation. Soft voice.)
Somethin' beautiful. Like the inside'a me. Beautiful ... The church wants that.

(The trumpet call begins and lights fade to black.)

FINAL CURTAIN

About the Author

A native of the South, DC Fidler has combined a career in academic psychiatry and cultural psychiatry with a lifetime of playwriting, acting, directing, composing music, and teaching creative writing and the dramatic arts.

He studied theatre, writing, chemistry, medicine, and psychiatry at the University of North Carolina at Chapel Hill, where he served on the faculty. He later served on the faculty at West Virginia University, teaching cultural psychiatry, clinical psychiatry, and acting.

A licensed psychiatrist, DC Fidler has lived and worked with the Alutiiq tribe in Akhiok, Alaska; the Al Moqbali Bedouin tribe near Sohar, Oman; the Kalkadoon Aboriginal Tribe in the outback of Queensland, Australia; and the Te Tau Ihu Maori Tribes on the South Island of New Zealand.

He began his acting career in outdoor dramas, summer stock theatre, and local films and television at age ten. He has written scripts and composed music for over fifty medical educational videos at UNC-CH and WVU. He has written twenty plays that have been produced in various community theatres and universities across North Carolina, Virginia, and West Virginia, as well as St. Louis, Sacramento, San Diego, Los Angeles, Boston, Chicago, and New York City.

He consulted and appeared in educational productions for HBO, ABC, and PBS and performed in numerous stage plays including: *Hope is the Thing with Feathers, Night of January 16th, Thieves' Carnival, Blood Wedding, Our Town, A Life in the Theatre,* and *Fool for Love.*

Presently, he is a scriptwriter, film director, and medical consultant for educational films using professional actors to demonstrate mental health issues. In addition, he is an active member of the Dramatists Guild of America and the Charlotte Writers' Club.

Fidler previously chaired the Video Committee for the American Psychiatric Association and served as President of the Association for Academic Psychiatry. In 2003, he was inducted as a Fellow of the Royal College of Physicians of Ireland. He serves on the Arts and Humanities Committee for the Group for the Advancement of Psychiatry where he is co-producing a video series on the History of Psychiatry.

He is author of the textbook, *Psychiatry for Actors: Using Psychiatric Principles to Build Characters,* and author of the novel, *Boogieban.*

Musicals by DC Fidler
- Pied Piper (With Lauren Horacek)
- Healer Man
- Medicine Show

Plays by DC Fidler
- Voices in the Woods
- Guilt by Association (With RJ Casey)
- Three Diaries
- Master William Bowlinggreen and Company
- Shiraz
- The Anniversary of Miss Nanette Pringle
- School Children Hiding Under Desks
- Grams
- Camp Uni
- Boogieban (Two-Actor Version)
- Boogieban (Seven-Actor Version)
- Ahulaqs
- Elk and Wolf (With Travis Teffner)
- Santee Delta (With Travis Teffner)
- Celtic Crossing
- Stone Touchin'
- Daugherty Park Merry-Go-Round
- La Dynastie
- Gyges Solution
- Begat

Short Plays by DC Fidler
- Persons
- Cruise
- Mobile to Where
- Oman Truce
- Second Amendment
- The Greek God Club
- Four X
- Microscopic Misconceptions
- Drone Guns
- Moon Bugs (With Travis Teffner)

Novels and Textbooks by DC Fidler
- Boogieban
- Psychiatry for Actors: Building a Character Using Psychiatric Principles